Flourish

Stepping out

and beyond ...

by
Katie Hawkins

Published by Peter Dawson
30 Elm Street
Borrowash
Derby, DE72 3HP

British Library Cataloguing-in-Publication data
A catalogue record for this book is available from the British Library

ISBN 978-1-8383404-3-8

Typeset by Carnegie Book Production, Lancaster
Printed and bound by Jellyfish Solutions Ltd

FLOURISH

This book is dedicated to my grandchildren: Grace, Lili,
Joe, Abi, Tom and Hope
who inspire me with their enthusiasm for life.

Contents

Changing Seasons

Consider the Birds

Listen For Your Name

All Change

Allelon (Gk)

Fit For Purpose

Waiting

The Cross

Contents

About The Author

The author is a wife, mother and grandmother to six wonderful young people. Now retired, she was previously a teacher and beauty therapist. She has been a preacher for almost thirty years and is married to a Methodist Minister. She enjoys mentoring and discipling, leading small groups and has pioneered community engagement in a number of locations.

In her spare time, she enjoys crafting, especially knitting and sewing for charitable causes.

You saw who you created me to be
before I became me!

Psalm 139: 16.
The Passion Translation

Introduction

During the Pandemic of 2020/21, I began to write a daily blog on Facebook, part journal, part devotional. As churches closed their buildings and Worship Services moved on-line, I asked God if I might ever preach again. He told me to work from home as many others were doing and so "Flourish" began. This publication includes a selection of posts from the blog all set in the context of restrictive measures including lockdown. Many of the discipleship principles mentioned can be applied beyond this season of restriction and difficulty.

God wants us to flourish in all circumstances. These posts contain hope, encouragement, challenge and some humour. They point us to a God who loves us completely in Jesus.

Throughout the book, there are spaces for you to add your thoughts and comments. You may want to write a prayer, a poem, draw – make these spaces yours. I hope that you will find this book an encouragement in your personal life as well as a useful discussion starter.

God Loves

Daisies!

On our walk recently we came upon a field with daisies, Spring is well and truly here.

I was reminded of a little rhyme that we said when playing as children: He loves me, he loves me not, he loves me, he loves me not. As we repeated the words, a petal was removed from the flower until the final petal remained. This petal determined whether or not love was in the air! Who the 'he' was depended, of course, on who the petal picker had in mind. According to my husband, boys didn't play this game.

This little rhyme has a long history, depending on what you read, and has nothing to do with being a follower of Jesus, just to be clear. God's love is not like this little rhyme. It does not change, it is not dependant on a final petal or whether God is in a good mood or whether He likes me or whether I have been good. God loves me!

God loves me and you. The English language only has one word for love and we can confuse its meaning and apply it inappropriately. God's love has its own word: *agape*. Agape is God's divine love. It is intentional, selfless, sacrificial and unconditional – there is no other love like it!

God Loves

Thank you, Father God, that nothing can separate us
from your agape love displayed in Jesus.

Safe Space

God's love surrounds us, we are safe in this love and in his will. If we go wandering off on our own path, protection is not guaranteed but God's love is everlasting. He is always looking out for us and waiting for us to return. God is protection. The Psalm writers tell us:

* But you are a shield around me. Ps. 3.
* As the mountains surround Jerusalem so the Lord surrounds his people. Ps. 125.
* In the Lord I take refuge. Ps. 11
* You hem me in – where can I go from you? Ps. 139
* He grants peace to your borders. Ps. 147: 14

I think God's love is like a spiritual hedge, keeping us safe. It keeps us enclosed in Him. The hedge of love gives us peace and space to flourish and to be fruitful. It protects us from disaster and evil. His love is our safe refuge. It is the very best place to be!

God Loves

Costly Love

God's love is deep, God's love is wide, God's love is high, God's love reaches out, God's love is faithful, God's love is powerful, God's love is forgiving. How have you experienced God's love in your life?

Paul, in his letter to the Ephesians, says that God's love surpasses knowledge. We can never know its full extent, it is expansive. You and I don't have a means of measuring this wonderful love, yet we can experience and know His love in Jesus. Jesus did not suffer and die on a cross so we might have an easy, carefree life. He died to bring us back to God; an horrific, painful death. We may have sung these words by Graham Kendrick: "How deep the Father's love for us how vast beyond all measure".

According to historical documents, early Christians were fed to wild animals or dipped in wax and set alight as lamps in Nero's garden. They suffered, because they spoke of Jesus as the only Lord and Saviour, the Crucified Christ, the Son of God. Today, Christians are persecuted around the world for their faith in Jesus Christ, this deep love is very costly. Religious freedoms are gradually being eroded, I pray our roots are deep in God and that we will stand firm. He will keep us when the day arrives.

Go Through it

There are times in our lives when we just have to grit our teeth and go through it. We call out to God "Help me!" We discover He does, looking back, we see His hand at work. The pain was real, the difficulties were real, but we just know He has been with us.

There is a wonderful children's story book by Michael Rosen, "We're Going on a Bear Hunt!" The children in the story face real challenges as they go hunting for the Bear: long grass, a deep cold river, mud, a dark forest, a snowstorm, the gloomy cave. At each obstacle they say these words, "We can't go over it, we can't go under it, we have to go through it!" They do, and get dirty, wet, bedraggled and very cold.

I wonder how many times I have looked for ways around the difficulties I have faced, rather than go through them to discover the God, who is always with me? God wants us rooted deep in Him so that we will get through to the other side one day. The front cover of Michael Rosen's book shows the children with their dad on the hunt. How much more is our Heavenly Father with his children. Whatever you face today, God is with you, it is a promise from Him to you.

Be blessed!

God Loves

Roots 1

For those of you who enjoy a pub quiz:

Question: Which tree has the longest root?
Answer: *Boscia Albitrunca* or Shepherd's Tree.

It is found in the Kalahari Desert, and has the longest documented tree root – over 70 metres! The story is that it was discovered accidentally, by workers drilling a hole in the desert.

This little story reminds me of a prayer in the Bible. Paul is writing a letter to a new church, he tells them he is praying for them, "I pray that you may be rooted and established in love". He wants the roots of their lives to be deep in God, in His love. When a root system goes beyond the shallow surface, when a root system goes deep into the ground, the tree becomes established – it is secure, it can hold and stand when the storms or droughts arrive. The roots find the nourishment deep in the ground when there is a drought. The root holds the tree secure when the gales blow. Life is precarious – let us pray that we will be rooted and established in God. Amen.

I just love that the common name for the tree is the Shepherd's Tree, Jesus is the Good Shepherd, any connection? I don't know but I would like to think so.

Roots 2

It is that time of year when clear plastic containers begin to appear in the warm airing cupboard and on window sills. It is seed planting season, did I tell you that we have an allotment? After a few weeks, these little seedlings will be planted in the ground, they can't stay in the warmth and comfort of the plastic tray on the sunniest windowsill. The roots will be restricted, becoming pot-bound and eventually the seedlings will die. The result will be no fresh veggies on the dinner plate or seed for next season's sowing. This isn't the plan for our allotment, we are expecting a bumper harvest!

Our faith journeys can be like this, we like the warmth and cosiness but after time we are pot-bound and we never become who God intends us to be. Being rooted in Jesus can mean struggle, not giving in, getting out there in a tough world, being hurt and misunderstood. The parable of the sower in Matthew 13 – the seeds sprang up quickly because the soil was shallow, but when the sun came up the plants were scorched, and they withered because they had no root.

Lord, I ask that I will have the courage to leave my cosy, warm life and search for the deep purposes of the new life you are offering me, a life of growth and fruitfulness. Grow my roots deep in you. Amen

God Loves

Keep On Keeping On

Think back to that day in March, 2020, when the Prime Minister told the country we were to stay indoors – locked down! I remember the feelings of shock and fear that swept through us all. How will we cope? If I get it, I'll die! Hand sanitiser and toilet rolls were like gold dust. I phoned my elderly Godmother of 96, she said, "It feels like the end of the world, it is eerie". Then she said, "We will just have to get on with it like we did in the war!" – and that is what we have been doing. There are days when even some politicians say how difficult and hard it is and they wish it was all over. It is tragic that so many have died, the whole world feels the grief of separation, this pain reaches us all and effects us all.

As followers of Jesus we are told to persevere, to keep going in the face of such life-changing difficulties. We return time and again to the challenge of the journey of this life, we cannot give up and shut down. Our hope is in God alone, our strength, our protector, our guide. Our God knows us and loves us, nothing, not one thing separates us from His love. He is Immanuel, God with us – I am so very grateful, are you?

Have a good day, keep on keeping on!

Your Space

Who Am I?

Friend

Jesus says you and I are his friends. Wow! Jesus, the Son of God, King of Kings, Saviour of the World says we are his friends. In John, Chapter 15, Jesus tells his disciples about the quality of this friendship. It is a friendship based on love and sacrifice. It is a friendship based on obedience to God's commands. It is a friendship based on the relationship between the Father and Jesus, "I have called you friends, for everything that I learned from my Father I have made known to you". Friendship is a relationship – a relationship where we can share openly and honestly; our feelings, our sadness, our needs and joys.

There is an old Victorian hymn which is a favourite of mine – "What a friend we have in Jesus", the words still apply today.

Abba

When we say "yes" to Jesus, we receive the Holy Spirit, we are 'born again' – it is very difficult to grasp. The salvation story in many ways is mystery. We believe and receive by faith, as we move forward in faith we get a glimpse of our new future as a child of God.

In the previous entry "Friend" we were reminded that we are Jesus' friends, now, we are reminding ourselves that we are children of God. John writes, "Yet to all who received him (Jesus), to those who believed in His name, he gave the right to become children of God, children born not of natural descent, nor of human decision or a husband's will, but born of God". Jesus encourages us to pray, "Our Father ..." The Holy Spirit assures us of this Father/child relationship, we know to whom we belong, we belong to "Abba, Father".

Some years ago, I was blessed to visit the Holy Land. Our flight out of Gatwick was full of Jews returning to Jerusalem for Passover. There were many families waiting to meet their men folk at the airport, the children ran forward calling, "Abba, Abba!" They were picked up, kissed and hugged by loving Abbas. It was a lightbulb moment for me, Abba had been an Aramaic word written on a page, I had never heard it in 'real life' nor had I seen the expression of it in context. God loves us, He is not distant, but close, immediate, welcoming and all embracing.

There is a wonderful worship song which goes like this:

"You unravel me with a melody, you surround me with a song of deliverance from my enemies till all my fears are gone.
I'm no longer a slave to fear, I am a child of God.
From my mother's womb you have chosen me
Love has called my name
I've been born again to a family, your blood flows through my veins.
I am no longer a slave to fear, I am a child of God."

You might like to look it up on Youtube.

Citizen of Heaven

Friend and child of God – this is who God says we are as believers. He also says that we are citizens of Heaven (Philippians 3:20). Heaven is our homeland, we often say that a person has "gone home, to be with the Lord" when they die. When we make the decision to follow Jesus, our status changes. We continue to live out this earthly life but the values we live by are those of the Kingdom of Heaven and our ruler is King Jesus. We have the Holy Spirit, the Bible and the fellowship of believers to help us make it home.

As believers, we now live as aliens and strangers in the world – we are passing through – 'on our way to Heaven' as the song says. We are pilgrims and travellers. Followers of Jesus hold dual nationality. Our earthly passports are issued by Governments of the world. Our Heavenly passport comes from faith in Jesus. Jesus has his Name on our Passport to Heaven, we enter our true homeland through Him. We wait expectantly for His coming and we live good lives, worthy of our King Jesus.

Co-worker

Friend, child of God, citizen of Heaven, co-worker, this is who we are. To co-work is to work with someone. Paul, in his letters, frequently addresses believers as fellow workers or co-workers with Christ.

A lovely little video clip popped into our phones last week, it was of our cute, great niece, Charlotte, who was helping her daddy clean the kitchen floor. Charlotte is 18 months old and was wiping away with her cloth while her daddy, on his hands and knees, did all the work!

Now here's the thing, daddy didn't need Charlotte to clean the floor, it would have been easier and quicker for him to complete the job himself. As he worked, he patiently encouraged Charlotte to help him. God our Father is like that with us, he encourages us to join in with his work. He doesn't need us at all, but the invitation to join in his work is for our good and not his. It is as we work with his encouragement that we learn the work of the Kingdom of Heaven.

Do you remember the story of Jesus feeding the 5000? The young boy brings his loaves and fish to the disciples, Jesus blesses the food – then Jesus says to the disciples, "You feed them". They work with Jesus to feed a very hungry crowd.

Who Am I?

Take time to consider what God, our Father,
is inviting you to.

Influencer

Friend, child of God, citizen of Heaven, co-worker with Christ and today, an influencer.

An influencer is now a recognised media career. Influencers have thousands of followers. By wearing a particular brand of trainers or clothing, by eating a particular food or drinking a certain beer, the influencer drives the market, they rarely advertise with words, they 'sell' a lifestyle on media platforms. Jesus says that we will be 'salt and light' in society, the equivalent of being an influencer. We are clothed in Christ, his light shines out from us; non-believers and believers are drawn to the attraction of the light in us. Followers of Jesus make a difference, our lives in Christ have power to change situations.

I read recently a description of how this works. Are you a thermometer or a thermostat? A thermometer tells us the temperature of the room, we might feel chilly, we look at the thermometer in the room and see immediately what the temperature is. Looking at the thermometer, however, doesn't change the environment, we are still chilly. On the other hand, a thermostat has the power to change the temperature, if the room is too cold, it will fire up the boiler until it reaches the required level of warmth. As followers of Jesus, we are set at Jesus. He alone is the mark on the thermostat

Who Am I?

of our lives, Jesus himself is the one who maintains us and keeps us so that our lives reflect him. I first became attracted to Jesus because I met a true Christian woman, she just "glowed" and I wanted what she had. Her influence set me on a journey.

Don't underestimate what God is doing in your everyday life as you follow Jesus.

Don't Be Afraid

Cleaning up

My dad's job was to wash the dishes after mam had cooked the Sunday lunch and then clean the oven. He did this every Sunday without fail. He also did other jobs – I might talk about them sometime! Cleaning the oven was one of the ways he served my mother and the family. Today, I am cleaning my oven, a job I don't enjoy at all! I have yet to find the perfect product and very occasionally I will pay a professional a large sum of money for the pleasure. I confess that it is several months since my cooker was last cleaned!

It has got me thinking about our lives, my life, how I need regular cleaning up. As Christians we are encouraged to confess our sins to God and each other so that we might be forgiven and healed. Growing up, I attended an Anglican Church where confession was said for sins of "ignorance, weakness and our own deliberate fault". I like that phrase, it helps me to get some understanding of sin. Sin separates us from God, it spoils our relationships – the dirt of our lives sticks. Those things we do or fail to do, the times when we have neglected God, the times when we have disobeyed and pleased ourselves; the wrong thoughts, the wrong words, the wrong actions all cast a shadow. Here is the most wonderful, amazing thing. God himself has provided the perfect solution for the enormous task of cleaning us up. The blood of Jesus cleanses us from ALL sin.

During the 2020 Presidential elections in the U.S.A. I heard that Donald Trump was considering giving himself a self-pardon, I laughed in disbelief but wait a minute – isn't there a part of me that would like to do the same? I make my excuses, blame others and circumstances. There is no self-pardon, God has pardoned us completely in Jesus, we are free to NOT sin, and when we do, we meet Him humbly and confess. He forgives everything of our past, present and future.

As I clean my oven, I will make it an opportunity to ask God about the things that need cleaning up in my life. What about you?

Forgiven

What did I learn while cleaning my oven? I learned not to leave it so long!

For 12 years, my husband, Rob, was Minister at a church in Newcastle-upon-Tyne. Over the years we held several nights of prayer – they were wonderful as we met with God. On one particular night, a large wooden cross was set up and people were invited to write on paper the things they were sorry about. There were nails and hammers for these regrets to be nailed to the cross. The sound of hammering went on through the night, it was very moving.

Paul says in one of his letters that Jesus forgave us all our sins, everything against us, Jesus took it away, nailing it to the cross. (Colossians 2: 13–14). He took it away! There is nothing that you can confess to him that has not been dealt with by his death. Nothing shocks Jesus. There is no need for us to carry around shame and guilt. We are free, cleaned up and ready to go with Jesus. We can say sorry to him at any time for anything.

Know his forgiveness today.

Live Ready

At a pandemic briefing Prof. Van-Tam, the Deputy Chief Medical Officer, was speaking about the developing vaccine. He talked to the media about the 'mum test'. I have already said to my mum, "Make sure when you are called you're ready". What he was saying was – don't have an excuse, get yourself prepared mentally, get organised so that you are free on that day and at the allocated time. I, your son, trust this is the right thing for you.

There are days when we are called by God to a specific task, sometimes we are ready, other times not. I am talking about the final call we will all receive, when Jesus returns. The preparation for that great and glorious day begins now, don't wait until it is too late! We will not get an emailed appointment date and time, we have to live 'ready'. Jesus says this in Matthew 24, "No-one knows about that day or the hour, keep watch, because you do not know on what day your Lord will come. You must also be ready, because the Son of Man will come at an hour when you do not expect him".

Be ready, ask the Holy Spirit to help you.

An Easy Life

There was great excitement in our house when my parents bought their first Oven Ready Turkey. I think my Dad especially, was relieved as it had been his job to deal with the turkey, feather plucking, innards, neck, head and all that this entailed. The Oven Ready Turkey was just perfect. So much time was saved as no preparation was involved.

Sometimes we treat our faith journeys like this, we want an easy life. We appreciate some good worship songs, we like an entertaining sermon, nothing too heavy or challenging, a message that pleases us, we like to feel good doing what is comfortable. We don't want to get too involved. But here's the thing, our faith journeys don't work like this, we have seasons of difficulty and it is just hard work. We have to persevere, digging deep into the little faith we have. Previously, I wrote about living "ready." The first verses of Hebrews 12 give us some pointers as how we can do this:

* We are surrounded by a great cloud of witnesses, believers who have done the journey, who are now with the Lord, they are willing us on to the finishing line. Cheering and shouting encouragement.

* Get rid of the bad stuff, it restricts us, Jesus died for all of it. We don't need it, it belongs on the tip!
* Persevere.
* Run your own race. (God has planned yours, don't try to run on someone else's track.)
* Keep your eyes on Jesus, keep following Him.
* Stay in training.

Come In Line

As a second lockdown is planned, we are assessing what worked for us the last time and how we might work smarter. We have learned a lot. As followers of Jesus, we are called to live differently, we are identified by the fruit of our lives: love, joy, peace, patience, kindness, goodness, faithfulness, gentleness and self-control. Of course, we cannot live this "different" lifestyle without the Holy Spirit working in our hearts, we need to ask for more of his power every day, we need to make space for him in our lives (Galatians 5:22).

Last week, Rob and I were decorating – that's a story for another day! My dad taught me to decorate. As a 16 year old, I had chosen a retro-style, flowery wallpaper for my bedroom. Dad produced a plumb line from his decorating tool-kit. "The plumb line", I was told, "is vital for getting everything straight and lined up, without it the flowers won't match. It will be a mess".

The prophet Amos was shown a plumb line (Amos 7:7), God was planning to use it to see how straight and true his people were to his commands and way of life. Jesus is the truth, He is our vertical point of reference just like the plumb line. I believe that in these difficult days we are called to get aligned with Jesus. Our own ways lead slowly and gradually away from Jesus. Have we drifted away over recent years and life is becoming a mess, I wonder? Now is the time to hear the call to come in line and stay close. Jesus loves you, He died for you!

Locked Down, Called Out

The words, *locked down, called out*, came to me as the second covid lockdown in England was announced. It came as a shock to many. It is one thing to go through something challenging once, but to do it again can feel just too much, can we bear it? I want to encourage you with these words: Don't be afraid, as God was with us in the past, He is with us now and will be in the future. We are called to believe not feel, a believer not a feeler. Feelings and desires can lie. Jesus and His word never lie. Trust Him.

Be the best follower of Jesus that you can be, ask for God's strength and help. Be the best neighbour / friend / boss / employee / student / parent you can be, ask God to help you. Tucked away in the many restriction guidelines is this, you may meet with one other person outside for a walk and chat on a park bench. Support each other. Pray in every situation you find yourself.

Your Space

Changing Seasons

Another Job for Dad

Every Sunday morning, after breakfast, we brought our shoes to dad for cleaning. I can see him now, sitting on a chair by the fire, newspaper laid out on the floor with our shoes, polish and brushes – I loved the smell of shoe polish. We only ever had 2 pairs of shoes, school shoes with sandals in the summer, and boots in the winter. Shoes were practical and for purpose, fashion didn't come into it, not like today!

I have been thinking about shoes. I love God telling Moses at the burning bush, to take off his sandals, because he is on Holy ground. I was once told of a Communion Steward who removed his shoes to prepare the Bread and Wine. There are times when worshippers remove their shoes as a sign of submission to a Holy God. Pilgrim travellers frequently walk barefoot.

In the story of Peter in prison, an angel comes from God to him and tells Peter to put on his clothes and his shoes, ready to escape. I love the verses in Isaiah which speak of beautiful feet that will bring Good News. And those verses in Ephesians which speak of the armour of God, the shoes of the gospel of peace which we are to wear. My favourite verse comes at the end of the story of the lost son, the errant son returns to his father, the father commands his servant to dress his boy in the best cloak, put a ring on his finger and shoes on his feet. A new beginning for this young man, where would his feet go next, I wonder?

Shoes speak of a life, they are sized to fit your foot, after a very short time, the leather moulds to the shape of your foot, they are the unwearable for anyone else. The wear on the heels and soles indicate how you walk. The wear also shows how far you have walked and the scuffs, dirt and marks show where you have walked. Jesus calls each one of us to follow him and he gives us what we need, he puts "shoes" on our feet so that we might go where he guides and leads. There are times when he calls us into new directions and has new tasks for us to do, new ministries and gifting, He will give us the "shoes" we need.

The seasons are changing, maybe you are feeling that God has a new role for you.

Are you ready?
March 8th 2021

We are making our first steps out of lockdown, beginning on Monday, March 8th with our children returning to school. I can imagine that parents and carers might discover that uniforms are still waiting to be washed, ironed or even found! (Bottom of school bags, under the bed!!!). If it has been hanging, pristine, in the wardrobe, will it still fit? (You know how quickly our young people grow!) Then there are shoes and trainers, do they still fit? What about the lunchbox? Let's hope it hasn't been left at school with the remnants of a last packed lunch – apple core, banana skin, half eaten sandwich, yoghurt pot, all quietly decomposing since before Christmas 2020!

In this time of change, we will encourage our children, we will help them to be ready. We will speak good things over them and make sure they are equipped for school in a physical classroom. In the same way, God our loving Heavenly Father is preparing us for change, He helps us, encourages us, speaks good words over us and equips us for a new season that is coming. He gets us ready – if we will let Him. Will you?

Some loving words from Father ...

The season has changed, the bondage of your barren winter has ended, and the season of hiding is over and gone. The rains have soaked the earth and left it bright with blossoming flowers. The season for singing and pruning the vines has arrived.

Song of Songs 2: 11–12 (Passion Translation).

Berlin

"Many small people who in many small places do many small things that can alter the face of the world" – a quote on the Berlin Wall Art Gallery. If today you are feeling small and useless. If today you are feeling overwhelmed by the enormity of the problems around the world. If today you are feeling trapped in circumstances and the restrictions of lockdown – talk to God, ask our Heavenly Father what small thing He wants you to do today and just do it. God, the Holy Spirit, will help you.

Back to Basics

All have sinned and fall short of the glory of God, yes all. To sin means to miss the mark and the mark is the glory of God. We can never be right with God and each other if we don't acknowledge the state of humanity which is missing the mark. Thinking positive thoughts is not going to put us right. There is a herd of elephants in the room! We ignore them because we don't want to be the first to say something, we don't want to upset people, we are embarrassed, our relationships are insecure, we keep quiet and dig deeper hell-holes by our silence. We leave those we love in ignorance of a Saviour who gave everything so that we can all make the mark.

In the story of the lost son, the boy ends up in a pigsty; many believers are climbing in the pigsty too as an act of solidarity. Yes, we are called to reach places of lostness – for the purpose of lifting up and pointing lost people to Jesus. It is right we care, but the greatest love we can show to the lost is to introduce Jesus to them.

I think it was John Major, a former Prime Minister, who adopted the phrase "Back to Basics". Jesus calls us to follow Him and tell others. It is simple. We have made it very, very complicated with our church programmes and projects. People are not programmes or projects!

Last night we were chatting to our youngest grandchild, we asked her what she thought she would do when the restrictions are over. "Well, I will probably just see my friends and chat". Let us be the believers who will see our friends to tell them about Jesus and what he has done for us.

Your Space

Consider the Birds

Birds

It is surprising how many varieties of birds are mentioned in the Bible. God made them all, he knows how they function and what they need to flourish. Jesus frequently talks about birds, drawing kingdom truths from their lives. In Matthew's Gospel, Jesus tells us not to worry. God knows what sparrows need, they don't fret or worry, their Heavenly Father provides all that these little birds need. Jesus says we are more valuable than the sparrows. What God does for the sparrow, He does for you and me. Isaiah says this, "He gives strength to the weary and increases the power of the weak. Even youths grow tired and weary, and young men stumble and fall; but those who hope in the Lord will renew their strength. They will soar on wings like eagles; they will run and not grow weary, they will walk and not be faint."

As a nation, we are weary of battling Covid 19. Individuals are exhausted by its physical and mental demands. The constant change of restrictions makes life difficult. Now is the time when we must live what we say we believe. These passages from Matthew and Isaiah bring us hope: God knows, God cares, God provides. You and I are precious to Him, so today, know your worth.

When we put our hope in God, we find strength, not just strength to survive but to rise up above the storm, to spread our wings and soar just like the eagle. Many years ago, we watched eagles soaring over The Rockies, they barely moved their wings, flying higher and higher until they were barely visible. Eagles know how to catch the thermals in the atmosphere, they expend very little energy and are magnificent to watch. I read recently that the only bird who will attack an eagle is a crow. It perches on the eagle's back, pecking at its neck. The eagle's response is not to fight the crow but to rise higher and higher until the crow falls off through lack of oxygen.

Today, put all your hope in God … you will rise, you will increase in strength. The burdens that you carry will fall away.

Hens

My husband, Rob, will tell you that I have always wanted to keep hens but every house we have occupied prohibited the keeping of wildlife. I don't think I am going to get my dream!

I know that many believers find real strength and comfort in Psalm 91. There is a verse which says this, "He will cover you with his feathers and under his wings you will find refuge: his faithfulness will be your shield and rampart". It speaks of God's protection and faithfulness. Small chicks are hidden away safely, warm and secure. God's protection is like this for us. Feathers are also waterproof, whatever is threatening to drown us will run off the protective covering that God provides. Be assured – we will not sink!

Jesus, in Matthew's gospel speaks over the city and people of Jerusalem, "I have longed to gather your children together, as a hen gathers her chicks under her wings". God longs to protect us, to gently hide us away in Him.

Thank you, Father, for your everlasting protection. Amen

Ravens

We have thought about sparrows, eagles and hens, this time, it is ravens.

When I first became a Christian, I was told that the story of Noah in Genesis was a myth, in fact little credence was being given to much of the Old Testament in those days! Jesus speaks of the days of Noah and he is found in the genealogy of Jesus, Noah was not a myth. Jesus is the truth and speaks truth. He doesn't lie!

Back to the ravens – they have purpose in God's creation, they are scavengers. They are often first at the roadkill today! They find food where they can. Noah sends a raven out of the Ark to "test" the situation, read it in Genesis 8. Noah understood the ravens and their purpose, to find food which, for the raven, is meat and other scraps. We read of the ravens later on in scripture. Elijah the Prophet, has spoken out against King Ahab. Ahab had married Jezebel, she worshipped false gods and had brought the idols into the House of Israel. Ahab had compromised his faith for this woman. God was angry. Elijah was sent by God to Ahab to tell him the consequences of his actions, a drought for several years. God then tells Elijah to hide away in the Kerith Ravine where there is a stream of fresh water. God also says this: "I have ordered the ravens to feed you there". So Elijah does as God tells him and the ravens bring him meat and bread for breakfast every morning and for his evening meal. Elijah is safe and the ravens provide his food. What does this little story tell us?

- * God is in charge of the whole of his creation.
- * God cares and provides for those who obey him.
- * God knows what we will need when we are engaged in His work.
- * God is ahead of us, he makes the task possible.
- * God won't be mocked.
- * Elijah hears God.
- * Elijah trusted God.
- * Elijah was obedient.

Lord, I ask that the truths in your word will become truths in my life. Amen.

Doves

Doves appear on Christmas cards, a symbol of the Prince of Peace. Doves appear on wedding cards, a symbol of love. Doves appear on sympathy cards, a symbol of comfort and rest. Baptismal, Easter and Pentecostal cards frequently feature a dove, a sign of the Holy Spirit being present and at work.

A dove features at very significant times in Jewish history. As I have studied these times, it has become clear that the appearance of a dove points us to new beginnings. We read in Genesis1 that the Spirit was hovering over the chaos. Artists for generations, have depicted this as a dove representing the Holy Spirit, present and actively waiting. A dove played a significant part in the story of Noah and the ark. It was the dove that brought back to Noah the first sign of life – a new leaf from an olive tree. It was time for a new beginning for the people of God.

The dove features prominently in the sacrificial system of the Jewish Temple. Doves were offered in Burnt Offerings, Sin Offerings and Purification Offerings. We read that Mary offered two doves for Purification after Jesus was born. These sacrifices brought some peace with God for a limited time until further sin needed covering by another sacrifice.

In Matthew and Luke, we read that Jesus comes to

the River Jordan to be baptised by his cousin, John. The Holy Spirit comes from Heaven like a dove and hovers over Jesus and God speaks, "This is my beloved son, in whom I am well pleased". A new beginning – this moment is recognised as the beginning of Jesus' Ministry. God is doing something completely new through his Son. It is Jesus who will bring us peace with God, He will be the sacrifice, the one and only. Jesus will be love in our hearts, Jesus will be comfort and rest. Jesus is our new beginning.

It is never too late to "begin again". Perhaps you have drifted away from Jesus, perhaps the circumstances of difficult days have got in the way of your friendship with Him. Are you losing the passion that you once had for Him? Do you long for a new start? Talk to Jesus, the only one who can give you new life.

My Son

We read what happened at Jesus' baptism. We learned that the Holy Spirit was over Jesus and that God spoke affirming words of identity and authority. Apparently, it was a common practice in those times for a Jewish father to present his son to the elders of the town with the words "This is my son …". This son of mine has my authority to do business on my behalf, he can make decisions, handle the finances, hire the staff, develop the business plan and more. For the people of those times, this proclamation over Jesus was profound and they understood what it meant. This must have been a wonderful experience for Jesus, to hear his Father confirm him. We know there were many others waiting to be baptised who heard, and we know from scripture that John heard these defining words and notes them carefully in his gospel.

Immediately, we read that Jesus is compelled into the wilderness by the Holy Spirit to face a testing experience. The first attack comes 40 days into this wilderness. Jesus is physically weak and hungry, Satan seizes the moment and says this, "If you are the son of God …" He challenges the identity of Jesus, trying to throw doubt into his mind. A tactic that he used with Eve in the Garden of Eden, "Did God really say?" A tactic also used today to trick us into doubt and disobe-

dience. The purpose is to steal our identity and under
mine our relationships with God and each other.

> *Know that you are a child of God. As a follower*
> *of Jesus your identity comes from knowing Jesus,*
> *you are found in Him. You are His child.*
> Read the account again in Luke, Chapter 4.

Tempted

He (Jesus) ate no food during this time and ended his forty day fast very hungry. It was then that the devil said to him, "If you really are the Son of God, command this stone to turn into a loaf of bread for you."

Jesus replied, "I will not! For as it is written in the Scriptures, Life does not come only from eating bread but from God. Life flows from every revelation from his mouth". Luke 4.

Resist

Is temptation a sin? What do you think? As I read my Bible, I am assured that the answer is no, BUT it can be very dangerous situation to be in! When we are faced with temptation, we have 2 choices:

* Resist it.
* Action it.

As believers, we will be tempted away from God's ways – we will come under pressure at our weakest point(s). Looking at the story of Jesus in the wilderness (Luke 4), we see very clearly how Jesus resisted the devil, the word of God – he quoted scripture to the devil. He used the word of God as a weapon (Hebrews 4:12). He stood his ground and did not give in – Jesus did not give in. He knew who He was, God's beloved Son, and He knew the word of God.

God, because He is so good and merciful helps us in all our weaknesses and temptations. He has given us an escape route – the living word, Jesus; and the written word, the Bible. Get to know Jesus more, get to know the Bible more – spend time with Him and His word.

Know that you are His!

Job Done!

There is always great satisfaction in saying these two words – 'job done'.

Previously, we thought about Jesus' baptism, this time we are looking at the role of John the Baptist. John was a prophet, he was a gift from God to his parents, Elizabeth and Zechariah. His name John means God's gift. He was born after many years of infertility and when Elizabeth was getting on in years. A miracle baby, it could be said, not unlike Abraham, Sarah and Isaac.

John was born with a job to do – you can read his job description in Luke 1: 76–79. On that day when Jesus was baptised by John, not only was Jesus confirmed, but John too! He would have had the assurance that he was doing God's will. Every word that he had preached, every person that he had baptised, every hardship of desert living, every shout of ridicule, the gathered food, the strange, rough clothing was all worth it. Every word that God had said came true at that moment, John 3:29–34.

It was almost 'job done' for John … but not quite!

Fake News

'Would I Lie to You?' Everything stops in the Hawkins' house when this programme comes on T.V. – Rob and I love it. Do you watch it? Two teams compete to tell stories, only one of which is true. The opposing team has to guess the true story. It's great fun!

Lies, distortions, fabrications are big issues in our society. It would seem that we find it very difficult to believe anyone or anything these days. Our hearts have become hardened, we are sceptical, cynical, selfish, over-protective and hypersensitive. We feel that no-one can be trusted. That's what lies do, they break down trust, destroy relationships, raise levels of anxiety and steal our peace. Jesus frequently said, "I tell you the truth". Jesus said of himself, "I am the truth". Where do lies come from? The Bible tells us that Satan is the source of all lies.

How do we live in these unbelieving days? We must make a choice to live close to the one who is truth, we will then be guided into the truth. Jesus will not fail us, Jesus does not lie to us, Jesus can be trusted. Let's hang on to this truth as life unfolds before us.

Your Space

Listen For Your Name

Reluctant Responder

– there are a lot of us around!

If you were brought up hearing the regular bible stories, at home, Sunday school, day school, kids' club or reading them yourself, you will know about Moses and the burning bush. You will remember the story, God speaks to Moses, calling him out of his regular routine of shepherding for his Father-in-law to go to Pharoah and ask for the Hebrews' freedom. How does Moses reply? Certainly not with a yippee and a resounding yes!

He has a catalogue of reasons why he shouldn't do as he is asked – Moses lives out a number of scenarios in a conversation with God around "What ifs". (Exodus Ch. 3). Finally, after many reassurances by God, Moses says he is not very good at speaking and please, would God send someone else (Ch. 4). God gives him Aaron, his brother, to help. God will teach them both and he will be with them. It's a great story. This God we worship will help us in our reluctance.

Be at peace – God is with us.

Reluctant Listener

Then there is Jonah, when he heard God calling him to go to Ninevah (modern day, Mosul, Iraq), he ran away, as far away as he could, getting on a ship sailing for Tarshish. (Possibly modern Lebanon or southern Spain, historians aren't certain). We know the rest of the story – storm, thrown overboard, swallowed by big fish, period of reflection and repentance, ejected on to the beach. God calls Jonah to go to Ninevah again, he goes and speaks, they repent, Jonah is peeved, Jonah sulks – because He knows God is good and that He keeps His word!

So often we think these stories are about individuals like Jonah and Moses, which to a certain extent they are. I believe they are more about God's character, his love and concern for people who are suffering. They are about rescue from slavery and oppression in Moses' case and saving from total wickedness and judgement in Jonah's story. God is good, He is patient and He wants all to be saved.

Another interesting observation: God calls individuals – ordinary, everyday followers ... YOU may be the answer, or a part of the plan that God has on his heart.

God Speaks

What is God saying to us in these very difficult days? To answer this question we must believe 3 things:–

* God does speak.
* He is always speaking.
* We have the capability to hear His voice.

The Bible says that God speaks through creation, through the prophets and through Jesus, the living word. I wonder how Father God is speaking to you today? Perhaps you will spend time in the beautiful, created world? You may read from the prophets or the words of Jesus? You may hear Him as you pray.

In these days of pandemic crisis for the world, we need to tune in to what God is saying to us as a follower of Jesus. What does He want us to do? Where does he want us to put our energy, resources and skills? What does He want us to know? To come through difficult situations, we need to hear his voice. We turn our attention towards Father God and ask him to help us to hear Him. When we do hear His voice, we are expected to be obedient to what He is asking of us, and believe what He says about us. There's an old gospel song: 'Trust and obey, for there is no other way – to be happy in Jesus but to trust and obey'.

It is always a good idea to make a note of what you sense God is saying to you. Keep a journal.

Hearing or Listening?

There are times when God speaks to us and we are not certain, we aren't sure of what we have heard, is this God? Could this be right? Was this really God or some fanciful idea of my own? At times like these, we can pray, asking God for more clarity, we can have a conversation with Him, just like Moses did on many occasions. We can share with a trusted Christian, seeking help and discernment. Perhaps you have a spiritual director, a mentor, a prayer partner or you belong to a small group. All of us need help and encouragement in our lives as we journey towards who God has created us to be.

I love the story of Samuel in the Old Testament (1 Samuel 3). He heard his name being called, he thought it was the old priest, Eli, calling him – it wasn't. This happened twice. Eli then realised that this was possibly God calling Samuel. Eli gives Samuel some advice: "If you hear your name again say, Speak, Lord, for your servant is listening".

I think there is a subtle difference between hearing and listening. For me, listening is intentional, it is paying attention to the one who is speaking. As followers of Jesus, we are listening for his voice amidst the noise of so many other voices. His is the voice that "rings true". You will never hear anything other than the truth from the voice of Jesus because He is truth. He frequently says in the Gospels, "I tell you the truth".

Keep listening!

Known By Name

In Bible times and even today, in the Middle East, sheep are brought into a fold at night. The fold is a circular holding pen, where they spend the night. These sheep belong to a number of owners but share one fold. One shepherd will stand as a security guard or sleep across the opening to prevent an attack from thieves or wild animals. Sheep are a precious commodity and shepherds all know their own sheep. Early in the morning, the shepherds will come to the fold and call their own sheep by name. The sheep will come to their shepherd – they recognise his voice, they won't go to a stranger's call. When the sheep have all responded to their shepherd's voice then the shepherd leads them out to safe places, to good grass, to quiet places, to water.

Jesus says, "I am the Good Shepherd; I know my sheep and my sheep know me". In these days of loud voices and chaos around the world, listen for Jesus – only he will lead you to safety.

Our picture was drawn by one of our granddaughters, she enjoyed watching the sheep in the field opposite our holiday cottage, interesting names!

Jesus knows you, He knows your name,
let him lead you.

Pay Attention Everyone

Jesus used a phrase a number of times when he was teaching his disciples: "He who has ears to hear, let him hear". In other words, he is saying pay attention to what I am saying, this is important! As a parent and a teacher, it has been necessary for me to follow up an instruction with this question, "Did you hear what I said, did you understand?" A question directed to the child or children who fail to listen and more importantly, do what has been asked. Children get very engrossed in their own activities. As God's children, we too get engrossed in our own concerns and we very often fail to hear God speaking to us.

Perhaps I don't expect God to speak to me, I'm not the Vicar, the Pastor, Minister or Leader, I'm not the professional church person! But hear this, we all have access to God through Jesus – as a follower of Jesus, you are made to hear Him. What He says is important. Sometimes listening just needs practice.

What ever you are doing – keep listening!

Your Space

All Change

Life Changing:
The Village

In John's Gospel, there is a story of Jesus sitting down by a well, he is hot, exhausted and thirsty. A woman from the nearby village comes to collect some water from this same well. Jesus strikes up a conversation and asks if she could get him some water. The conversation continues around issues of race, gender, lifestyle and worship. The woman talks about waiting for the Messiah. Jesus says to her, "It's me!" She runs back to the village and to tell everyone to come and meet Jesus. Some of them do immediately, others invite Jesus to stay for a couple of days. Jesus shares with them and they, too, believe. An encounter with Jesus is life-changing, not only was the woman in our story changed but many Samaritans were transformed because of her invitation to meet Jesus. (John 4).

There are many Alpha Courses available throughout the year. You could invite someone, or sign up yourself, if you need a reminder of who this life changing Jesus is.

The free gift of God is eternal life, He is a life changer!

Life Changing:
The Household

Think about your life, how has being a follower of Jesus changed you? What have been the pivotal moments? The key people who told their stories? The Bible words that burned deeply into your heart? The song that took you into that place of worship? The prayer answered?

There was a young boy who was very ill, he was dying. His dad was a high ranking official in the Royal Palace – he comes to Jesus and asks him to help his son. He asks Jesus to come to see the boy. Jesus declines the invitation but says this, "You may go. Your son will live". The Father takes Jesus at his word and sets off home to find the boy recovered at the exact moment Jesus had pronounced "Your son will live."

The words of Jesus are powerful. In this story, not only is the boy made well but the whole household then believed in Jesus. We heard of a village changed, now it is a whole household. Just imagine what that village and household looked like after this meeting with Jesus. There is a verse in this story that has really challenged me – 'The man took Jesus at his word and departed'. John 4:50.

To take Jesus at his word and put action in line with Jesus' word is life changing.

Life Changing:
From a Taker to a Giver

Paying taxes has never been popular. The collection of taxes has seemed a heavy, unfair burden for some when others find ways to "fiddle the books!" There is always controversy around taxes.

Zaccheus was a tax collector working in Jericho. The word went out that Jesus was coming. Zaccheus, so the story says, was a short man, the children's song says he was a very little man. He closed his roadside office and ran to a nearby tree, climbed it so that he could see Jesus from this vantage point, never dreaming that Jesus would see him! Jesus calls Zaccheus down and invites himself to his home. Others, more tax-collectors and undesirables, join the meal at Zaccheus' house with Jesus. In Jesus presence, Zaccheus is changed. He promises that he will give half his possessions to the poor and IF (?) he has cheated anyone he will repay them four times over, double the amount required by the law. Zaccheus becomes a follower and a dramatic change occurs – a taker becomes a giver.

To give is to reflect the nature of God, God gives generously. He gives us his Son, Jesus. We know that everything we have comes from God. Freely we have received, freely we give. We are encouraged to give generously to the poor of the world.

All Change

The name Zaccheus means righteous one, pure, innocent. On that day when he met Jesus, Zaccheus became who he was intended to be, now isn't that just amazing?

Allelon*

* from the Greek

Servant

We are hearing amazing stories of ordinary people doing extraordinary things during this pandemic. We heard of one retired nurse who is organising one of the large vaccination centres in the Midlands. We know of Street Pastor friends who are supporting the medics and public in another centre. We know of teams of people sewing who have been making face masks and scrubs. We know of people giving their time to feed the hungry and provide clothing. The stories are many. These people are not famous, they are ordinary men, women and children giving what they have of themselves for the good of others, the world will never know their names. We are very thankful for such lovely people.

There are two kinds of volunteers, those who draw attention to themselves and those who draw attention to the needs of the suffering and do something about it. Sometimes you will hear of someone famous, they are marked with qualities of humility and integrity. They use the fame to serve, it helps the work, the fame serves the serving. We see that very thing in folk like Marcus Rashford and Bill Gates – they use their name, fame and wealth in serving, it opens doors and gets the job done. Jesus came to serve, He is volunteer number 1!

"He made himself nothing, taking on the very nature of a servant being made in human likeness ... he humbled himself". Philippians 2

Free to Serve

We have thought about people who volunteer and serve others. Towards the end of his ministry on earth, Jesus washed his disciples' feet, not a very pleasant task. It was usually carried out by the lowest servant in the household, a non-Jew and probably a slave. Some of his disciples were horrified, especially Peter!

There's a sentence in John's Gospel which goes like this, "Jesus knew that the Father had put all things under his power, and that he had come from God and was returning to God". Jesus KNEW! Jesus knew who he was and where he was going. Jesus knew that all things were under His power, some translations use authority or feet. This identity and authority was announced at His Baptism. Jesus heard the voice of God, together with the Holy Spirit's presence confirming him as the Father's son and equipping him with power and authority. His identity as God's Son set Him completely free – to serve, to wash feet and surrender his life on a cross.

It is God's love for you that gives you identity. It isn't wealth, title, academic achievements, fame, skills or achievements but His love for you that sets you free. Today, know that you are a loved son or daughter, that you are free to serve.

"Here I am, Lord, send me". (Isaiah 6:8)

New Vocabulary

'Oneanothering'?

It is amazing how many verses there are in the New Testament that include the phrase one another, some spoken by Jesus, others are found in the letters written to new believers by the apostles. Verses such as love one another, encourage one another, speak to one another in spiritual hymns etc, serve one another, respect one another, honour one another, admonish one another, the list is long. In the English language, one another, are 2 words, in the original Greek, there is only one word, 'allelon' which contains within its meaning 'one another each other'. It emphasises a greater mutuality of relationship than the English phrase. It is a richer, deeper word that expresses a quality of relating between believers.

'Oneanothering' is how we relate to each other, we are created for relationship with God and with each other. Jesus has the perfect relationship with the Father, Father has the perfect relationship with Jesus. The relationship brings glory to the Father and to Jesus, there is total mutuality, each honours the other. We are familiar with words such as mothering, parenting, fathering, teaching, ministering. Let us as Jesus' followers be engaged in 'oneanothering'.

Your Space

Fit For Purpose

Repurpose

During lockdown, many friends were posting great pictures on their daily exercise walks. God, the Holy Spirit, often speaks to me on my walks and I have started to take photos of those moments and places. God wants to teach us about life with him as we travel on this earth. My current conversation is about repurposing. I have been surprised by how many buildings have been repurposed in my area. For example: there's an old girls' school just across the road from our home – it is now a private house, there's a micro-pub, once a bank and a former church building is now repurposed into apartments.

Is God wanting to repurpose me? Is He wanting to repurpose you? Perhaps you and I need a refit for purpose? Many of us have become comfortable in our discipleship journeys, we like what we like and we worship and serve, all within our comfort zones. Heaven forbid that we might have to leave that comfort zone! Last week, I heard a speaker ask, are we worshipping a God of cosiness or a God of holiness? Has the Almighty become the all-matey as my husband often says.

God is a Holy God, there is no-one like him. Maybe the question needs to be asked – cosiness or holiness?

Repurposed by The Builder

Jesus says, "I will make you into fishers of men."
Jesus says, "I will build my Church."

Repurposing requires that we leave the familiar, the comfort zone where we are safe and in control to 'go' to another place. When we do move out, we face certain feelings that we don't like: fear of failure, lack of self-confidence, increased sensitivity, we become affected by others' opinions, we begin to find excuses to stay where we are. It's safe and we are in control. Moses had plenty of excuses – so many what ifs! Many of us are just the same if we're honest. All of this reluctance denies the Lordship of Christ in our lives.

We know that some churches are facing threat of closure for many reasons, not just the pandemic, although this has hastened the day. Those places where we have worshipped, where our marriages took place, where children were baptised and so much more, those buildings may prove to be unsustainable over the coming months and years. We know that the church is people, together, worshipping God and serving our communities. We do have sentimental feelings for our buildings, they have been our 'nesting places' as an old lady once said to me. This time of repurposing may be unwelcome by some but it is happening. Jesus is Lord, he will build his Church and he will make us into the people God is creating us to be.

It is good to remind ourselves that the first followers of Jesus and the early Christians met in people's homes – sharing food, praying for each other and retelling the story of Jesus.

Health Warning

A couple of years ago I went to my regular hairdresser in Newcastle. She was not very happy, a rather large lady had sat in the salon chair and it had broken. Thankfully, the lady was unhurt. I had to laugh when my hairdresser went on to say, "I blame the leggings!" I know what she meant, leggings and joggers are so easy to wear. They are comfortable, the elastane stretches and there is no awareness of the extra inches going on here and there. Tailored trousers would warn us of increased weight and the possible risk to health. Perhaps this is a good time to go through my wardrobe?

It is so easy, in our faith journeys, to become comfortable. Jesus gives us freedom – freedom to go where we want and do what we want. We are given freedom to choose, the choice is ours. Some choices that we will make, however, are contrary to God's will. Wrong choices have consequences and like stretchy leggings, eventually they will tell! God gifts us with freedom, it is an expression of His love for us. The death of Jesus sets us free to not sin and to follow Him.

The safest place we can be is within the will of God. In that safe place we can experience complete freedom. His hand is on us, we are safe. Psalm 139: 5–12

Spiritual Fitness

I hated P.E. at school, it is not my thing! I didn't like getting sweaty, I didn't like the extra effort, I didn't like jumping and climbing over things that were bigger than me, I didn't like being pushed, I didn't like the feeling that I might fall and get hurt. You get the message, I didn't like it, I still don't!

No one needs to buy me a Fit Bit for a present, I know what it will say!

Spiritual disciplines help with our spiritual fitness. We need to strengthen our inner core, our inner being as a believer, it is an inside job! One discipline is prayer, I am sure we all "say our prayers", we have lists of people and situations to pray for.

When Jesus lived on the earth, he prayed regularly to his Father in Heaven. The disciples saw him praying and asked Jesus, "teach us to pray". Praying was how Jesus stayed close to His Father. It was how their deep relationship was kept alive, it was how they communicated, it was how Jesus was able to live on the earth – it was a relationship that connected heaven and earth.

If the first followers of Jesus asked him for help with this, then we can ask too.

Lord, teach me to pray – take me beyond endless lists.

Speaking and Listening

Prayer is the place where our relationship with God is nurtured and deepened. It is vital to our journey that we listen to God and hear what he is saying. Jesus said, "I only do what I see my Father doing". Jesus also tells us that the Holy Spirit speaks only what he hears. I think, if I'm honest, it is very likely that I have wasted an awful lot of time and energy over the years because I wasn't listening and not hearing what God was saying. It is also a possibility that if I did hear, I chose not to do it. I am so thankful that God is very patient and forgiving, aren't you? We all need to hear his "voice". God is always speaking, we need to become familiar with the ways he speaks to us, to recognise that it is indeed him.

A listening exercise:

1. You will need a pen and a blank piece of paper.

2. Thank God that he is with you, ask him to speak to you.

3. Wait (it will be a challenge, initially).

4. Write down or draw what you sense or see or hear.

You may hear words of a song, see a picture, get an impression, words of scripture, a name, God speaks in many different ways.

You may not have anything to record at first, but God often surprises us with something later. He doesn't live to our timing!

Keep listening!

Fit For Purpose

Settled Quietness

Our friend, Coralie, a young mum with four small children had a "prayer chair". Susannah, John Wesley's mum, sat with an apron covering her head and face whilst her large family were around her. These two mums were in the place of prayer; when their children saw this, they were trained not to interrupt. Mummy's praying. Jesus frequently went to a quiet place to pray.

In our busy, distracted lives, it is necessary to intentionally find the quiet place – not only a physical space but a settled place of quietness within our core being. We are to find the place where we can speak and listen to God our Father, without distraction. If Jesus needed to do this, then we do too!

I really need to pay attention to this, Lord, because in paying attention to this I am giving my attention to you, help me. Amen

Prayer of Command

Today, I sense that God wants me to share with you the prayer of command – a way of praying when we are in difficult circumstances, when the storms of life threaten to overwhelm us. You remember when Jesus was sailing with his disciples? He was asleep and a storm blew up, the disciples were terrified and woke him. Jesus commanded the storm "Quiet!" "Be Still!" On another occasion, Jesus tells his disciples that if they have faith they will tell mountains to move into the sea! These same disciples had heard Jesus curse a fruit tree, they had seen it shrivel and die.

After Jesus had returned to Heaven and the Holy Spirit had been given to the disciples, Peter and John came across a disabled man begging. They speak to him, tell him that they haven't got any money but what they do have they give to him – in the name of Jesus Christ of Nazareth, "Stand up and walk!" Jesus encourages believers to pray in his name, he gives believers authority to use his name – Jesus Christ of Nazareth. He tells his disciples to "Go in my name". There is power in His Name. It is a powerful name, the name high over all. The world is facing an enormous mountain, living in the storm of a pandemic with so many lives lost. Pray this prayer with me, if your faith allows:

In the name of Jesus Christ of Nazareth, I speak to Covid 19 and command you to shrivel and die. Amen

The Secret Place

Tucked away in the Sermon on the Mount (Matt. 6: 1–18), Jesus teaches his disciples about three spiritual disciplines: giving, praying and fasting. He warns them strongly about "showing off". He frequently accused the pharisees of this and tells the disciples that they are to give "in secret", they are to pray "in secret", they are to fast "in secret". All of this directs us to an internal work that is seen by God alone. In the "secret place" our reward is God, himself – it is a moment of intimacy and a connection of two hearts. He is our greatest reward. In our weakness, we long for recognition and acknowledgement from men and women, we really battle with this. We want to be the best, we want to be seen and we want to be known.

I learned that one of the criteria for ordination laid down by John Wesley was fasting on Wednesdays and Fridays! I don't think it is on the list today! He saw it as a valuable means of spiritual growth. All spiritual disciplines are a means of bringing the believer closer to Father God, so that he may continue to transform us into the likeness of Jesus.

Lord, help each one of us to "grow up" in Jesus.
Help us to leave behind the things that get in the way.
Help us to know you in the "secret place". Amen.

Share Together

So, who will we be and what will we do when this is all over? Now there's a question!

I meet every Tuesday with a friend in Newcastle – by phone, we share about life, we share what we sense God is doing in these times, we share scripture and we pray. Together, we are convinced that the Holy Spirit is doing deep things in the hearts of people and in us. I have just finished a small group meeting on zoom, we meet every Thursday, we share about life, we share what we sense God is doing with us in these times, we share scripture and we pray, together. God calls us into relationship with him through Jesus, and into relationship with each other. There are deep needs that can only be met in relationship. We are created to be together, firstly with God, he is our Father. Jesus, related in everything to his Father. Jesus had his small group – Peter, James and John – then a larger group of disciples.

We all need people with whom we can share life, find encouragement; trusted people with whom we can be honest and open, people who will speak kingdom life into us. We need believers who will watch over us, who will have our backs. There is a before and after story going on – we haven't got the picture yet – but God is mightily at work!

Encouragement

I don't know if this is a recognised spiritual discipline but it certainly should be. We got a text from a young person living in Manchester this morning on her way to school, 'life's a bummer!' A strong reaction to the announcement that the city was going into tier 3 restrictions in the pandemic battle.

Paul wrote many letters to Christians around the Mediterranean. They are full of encouragement and thankfulness. Believers all over the world need encouragement, to know that they are loved and are prayed for, to be told that God is good and that He is with us. We know that many of our friends and family are struggling, young as well as old – life is a 'bummer', it isn't easy at the moment. For many people this situation is very frightening. I wonder when we last got in touch with someone, a message, a text, a letter or card, a phone call? Encouraging each other is much needed – let's just do it. Have a good day and know that God is for you, He is our greatest encourager.

Bible Reading

Why do we read the Bible? There are many reasons: it is the word of God, it teaches us how to live, it introduces us to Jesus, it gives hope, it gives challenge, it tells us about the character of God, it is His Story. The Bible tells us where we fit in, where we belong, it is food for the soul and more. It tells us that we are loved and God has plans for us, good ones. The word of God is alive and active, it has power to transform us, our families, our churches, our nations – if we will believe it. So often our Bible study has become little more than a comprehension exercise. We need to take Jesus at His word.

In our small group the topic of free school meals came up. A decision by the Government to withdraw free school meals during half-term caused a strong reaction amongst us. Within a few hours, a voucher scheme was set up and available for those who needed extra food for the family. We took action! As disciples, Jesus clearly gives us the responsibility, he says to his disciples, "You feed them". Many churches are actively involved in Food Banks and in cooking and delivering food to those who need it.

The word of God informs our actions as believers, as James said in his letter: 'Faith without action is dead!'

The Challenge of Spiritual Discipline

Bible Study is alive – active – eye-opening – relational – engaging – motivational – connecting – announcing – proclaiming – lamenting – loving – expansive – transforming – sharing – feeding – refreshing – fulfilling – guiding – comforting – speaking – building – resting – growing – renewing – working – correcting – training – teaching. We experience many of the above as we read, we also get to know God's nature and character. We are introduced to Jesus. We are invited to meet Jesus, the Living Word, to receive Jesus and know Him and join Him in the Kingdom of Heaven. He invites us, let us always be saying "yes"! Many non-believers meet Jesus for the first time reading one of the gospels by themselves in their own home.

If you are feeling out of touch with Jesus can I encourage you to read through one of the Gospels. Probably Mark is best because it is the shortest! It is fast moving and gathers the reader up into the person of Jesus.

Best Seller

On Annual World Book Day – I wonder if many Bible characters will be on show? Who would I be? Would I choose to be one of the good guys or perhaps I might be one of the wicked ones? Which character might you choose to be?

The Bible is a genre of its own. Presented in book form – its words are not bound – they live – and give life. They give insight to the nature and character of God, the words speak of His ways. We read it, prayerfully asking God the Holy Spirit to guide us, teach us and to take us into mysteries we will never fully understand. Every time we open its pages we enter another world. If we dismiss its contents, if we deny its truth, if we put it on the shelf to gather dust along with every other book – then we are impoverished. We miss out on so much of what God has planned for us.

Some words for us to consider from a long recognised "Best Seller":

'I have hidden your word in my heart that I might not sin against you'.

'I have put my hope in your word'.

'Your word, O Lord, is eternal; it stands firm in the heavens'.

'Your word is a lamp to my feet'.

'All your words are true'.

'The unfolding of your words gives light; it gives understanding to the simple'.

(All from Psalm 119).

Be Blessed in your simplicity!

Fishy Friday!

I wonder how many of you eat fish on Fridays? It is on our menu! When teaching early years children the days of the week, it was 'Fishy Friday'. We always had fish for school lunch on Fridays so it was easy to learn and remember. Eating fish on Fridays has its origins in fasting, a preparation for confession and repentance. Early years children knew nothing of this, they just enjoyed the fish fingers!

The Advent season is traditionally a fast season, preparing believers for the Feast of the Nativity. It is a season of simple food, reflection and spiritual preparation; certainly not shopping, parties and decorations. A season of waiting for the coming of Christ, not only at his birth but His final coming as King of Kings. I read recently that many believers are rediscovering the purpose of Advent and are intentionally engaging with the Advent fast. Perhaps the pandemic restrictions have lifted us out of the frantic, secular days of Christmas preparation. We have been given an opportunity to engage with Advent and what it means for those who follow Jesus. Seasons of fasting such as Advent and Lent are not about what we might give up but what we gain by having walked through the season.

The feast is always more joyful after the fast!

Fall on Your Knees

Over the Christmas period, the song "O Holy Night" had been on my mind. Whenever Rob and I passed each other going about the house, we were humming or singing this song. Then we began to notice that many Christmas Services included, you've guessed, "O Holy Night", then a Christmas card arrived with the words, "O Holy Night". They were singing it in Birmingham, Watford, Manchester, Newcastle, Australia and America. God speaks to us in many ways, he was certainly very persistent with this song. I ended up downloading the lyrics, playing and singing the song MANY times. I am sure our lovely neighbours also know it well by now!

What are you saying to us God? The climax of the first verse moved us powerfully, 'Fall on your knees'. Could this be what God was saying? We must learn to worship again. We must position ourselves in an attitude of worship, first and foremost. The first Commandment calls us to put the worship of God as our priority – nothing else must take His place.

When we read the birth of Jesus, we see that the Angels worshipped, the shepherds worshipped, the wise men worshipped. Jesus, the Son of God was born, surrounded by worship. Saint Richard of Chichester prayed these words, "May I see thee more clearly. Love thee more dearly and follow thee more nearly, day by day". Saint Paul wrote in a letter that he resolved to know only Jesus Christ. Let us resolve to put God first and last. Any other resolutions we might make will fall in order, or disappear if they don't align with God's plans.

Your Space

Waiting

Get Off The Bus

I have been praying about what God wants me to share with you. Many of you, I know, are back in restricted measures or are isolating. Some of you are anxious about education, many are concerned about finances, employment and health. These are hard times, in it all God knows and is with us – lean into Him. Many Christian fellowships are praying about how they can bring the hope of Jesus into their communities. "What do you want us to do, Lord, show us?" is the question.

Picture an open top, sightseeing tour bus, I sensed the Lord saying that the days of sightseeing through life has to change. We can no longer sightsee through the parts of discipleship that are easy, pleasurable and appeal to our personal taste or fit in with our earthly lifestyle. We can no longer pick the parts of the Bible that we like. We are to wrestle with the verses that feel uncomfortable and challenge the prevailing mindset. I sense that we are to stop hopping on and off, visiting the latest "good idea" that pops up. We are to stop being sightseers. We are to get off this tour bus and find the way that will take us to the place where God wants us. In these days keep asking for His guidance. God Bless you in your search!

Giraffes

I love giraffes. We visited Twycross Zoo during the Summer with our granddaughter and spent time watching them in their enclosure. They are special to me because they remind me of something I was told as a new Christian. A lady who was discipling me told me to learn to pray like a giraffe. A giraffe has a far reaching view of their surroundings, they look from a different perspective. There are times when we get so taken up with our own problems and difficulties, we barely lift our heads to see what else is going on, or step back and away to get a fuller perspective. We must learn to rise up, lift up our heads and see the bigger picture and to where God is directing our gaze. The Bible gives many pointers, here are two of them:

* We know the way will be narrow, we will have to search for it. The way will not be obvious but it will be in line with the word and will of God. (Matthew 7: 13–14.)
* It will involve serving and helping the poor, the hungry and thirsty, the sick, prisoners and homeless as well as those who have insufficient clothing. (Matthew 25: 31–46)

This is certainly not a sightseeing tour!

The Bus Stop

The entry *Get Off The Bus* (page 114) resonated with many. If you have made a decision to stop riding on the sightseeing tour bus, if you have "got off" the bus, I sense that there will be those on the tour bus who will try to pull you back on board, this will be the testing time. You are entering the waiting time, don't be afraid but stay waiting. Pray in your waiting, watch in your waiting and listen in your waiting. Then you will see the way to take. There is a bus stop round the corner from our home, no route number, no timetable, no destination – our time of waiting will feel like this but stay and wait.

Waiting Place

Waiting is often perceived as a waste of time. A dead time when nothing seems to be happening, "occurring" as Ness says on Gavin and Stacey.

To wait in the waiting place is certainly not that, it is an attitude, a status of being, it is how we find ourselves in chaotic days. I am certainly one of those who has got off the sightseeing tour bus and am waiting for the new thing that God is going to do in my life and the life of believers.

Have you ever stood in the check-in queue at the airport when a traveller in front of the queue has an overweight suitcase? They open the case and start to off load what is not needed and we inwardly sigh! In these days of waiting, I sense that God lovingly sighs and says to us, "You will have to leave some of this stuff behind, you don't need it, it is weighing you down and taking up space for the new things I am going to give you". There is no room for excess luggage on the new bus. Let's begin to ask God what he wants us to leave behind.

Remember when Jesus sent the first disciples on mission, he told them to travel light, no bag, no extra clothing, shoes, no cash. Why did Jesus say this? When we take our own resources we are self-sufficient, we don't need God. We are independent. God wanted the disciples to know that he would provide as they travelled.

He wants us to know that too, we can depend on Him, He is everything we need. He is "God Provider".

Lord, as I wait, I am willing for you to sort out the suitcase of my life, show me what is excess baggage.
Amen

Waiting Patiently

I am not very patient – my husband will tell you! Sometimes things are just too slow!

There's a story in the Old Testament of Abraham and Sarah. Here's a summary: both were old, they had no children, God promised them a child and from that child there would be as many descendants as the stars in the sky. They both laughed at that idea! Years passed by and still no baby, their patience was running out. Sarah had a servant girl, she gave the girl to Abraham as a wife (more than one wife was acceptable at the time). Abraham was quite happy with this arrangement, he didn't say 'no'! A baby boy was born but not to Sarah! This was not the promised baby God had in mind. Further years passed and Sarah did have the promised baby, Isaac, just as God had promised. Some thoughts from this story:

* When God says he will do it, he does.
* Be patient and wait.
* Don't manipulate people.
* Resist the temptation to rush and work it out for yourself.
* God is God!

The Waiting Time

I wonder how you get on in a time of waiting? I hope that you are able to view it as a gift, an opportunity to spend time praying and asking God, "What next for me?" There was a wonderful Art Exhibition in Newcastle Cathedral of works produced in a local prison. One exhibit was a beautiful textile cross, crotched with cottons in many colours, it looked beautiful and was well produced.

The Crucifixion of Jesus, we know, was nothing like this. It was cruel, painful, violent and bloody. I remember the first time I saw Mel Gibson's, "The Passion of The Christ", I turned away, I couldn't bear to look. Many historical accounts verify the facts of crucifixion, it was and still is the cruellest form of execution. Matthew, Mark and Luke all mention these words that Jesus said to his disciples, "If anyone would come after me, he must deny himself and take up his cross daily and follow me." Luke 9:23.

Could it be that in this waiting time we are being challenged by the Cross and Jesus' sacrifice?

Jesus denied himself to obey his Father so we might travel home to Father's house and have access through the front door of Heaven. Jesus has paid the cost.

Your Space

The Cross

We Are Changed

June 21st, 2021 was the predicted date for the end of covid lockdown restrictions. The date when every door would be open and we would be free. We would have to open our personal front doors, assess the damage and look to rebuild our lives and communities.

There was a moment when Noah had to leave the ark, he had to physically open the locks, look out, walk out, assess the situation and start to rebuild. There was a moment when Joseph and Mary had to leave the stable with Jesus, and re-enter a country ruled by an unpredictable tyrant, King Herod and the terrorising roman occupation. When we open our doors, are we ready for what is waiting for us "out there"? I pray I am.

I read a headline a few months ago it said this: 'IN THESE UNKNOWN TIMES, KNOW YOUR TIMES'. What is God asking us/me to do in these times? Are we ready to step out into the hurting world and to step up to what God is asking of us? I think we are going to be surprised for we are changed!

The Key Code

Many buildings are now secured with key pads, a code is given to those who need to know so that those people can come into the premises freely. In my last "paid" role, the key codes were changed regularly on gates and entrance doors to the school, just in case the code had been shared with the wrong person. Jesus says about himself, "I am the gate; whoever enters through me will be saved. He will come in and go out and find pasture. The thief comes only to steal, kill and destroy; I have come that they may have life, and have it to the full". (John 10:10.)

Much has been stolen from us by the pandemic, many have died and a familiar way of life has been destroyed for thousands. Jesus has come so that our lives might be filled with the fullness of himself, we hang on to this as Jesus' followers. Many are telling me that they feel closer to Jesus now than they did before Covid 19 entered our shores. Jesus is the gate and he is also the key, what Jesus suffered on the Cross, his brutal death, his sacrifice opened the gate to the Kingdom of Heaven and the hope of eternal life. The key code doesn't get regularly changed, the entry code is set permanently at the Cross of Jesus.

The Rubbish Tip

"There is a green hill far away, outside the city wall" goes the first line of a hymn that is traditionally sung on Good Friday. The place on which the crucifixions took place was no green hill but the rubbish tip for Jerusalem. It was an open landfill site known as Golgotha, outside the walls of Jerusalem. It had been the local quarry according to archaeologists but was now used for the purpose of rubbish disposal. Can you imagine what it looked like and smelt like?

Jesus was crucified to put us right with God, he took all the sins of the world into his body so that the we might be sin free. He was and is "the Lamb who takes away the sin of the world". In Hebrews 12, we are encouraged to throw off every thing that gets in the way. The sins that we fall into (because we are still human) are forgiven, we say sorry to God and continue the race of life – these failures, bad habits, wrong thoughts, lifestyles and selfishness no longer have power to restrict us. Throw them way – you are free to do that. It is very humbling to know that the Son of God took all the rubbish of this world to the rubbish tip of Jerusalem because God loves us so much.

Reconciled

God is God, there is no one like him. His ways are not our ways and we can never understand, we just have to say, "I am trusting you". It always amazes me and humbles me that God entrusts his followers with so much: telling the story of Jesus, the making of disciples, baptising new followers and teaching them to be obedient followers. God's desire is that all people and creation will be reconciled to himself, "all this is from God, who reconciled us to himself through Christ and gave us the ministry of reconciliation". (2 Corinthians 5:18.)

God has entrusted us with the ministry of reconciliation! We are entrusted to tell this amazing story that there is no longer any barrier between us and God, our sin is taken away, no more guilt or shame, no condemnation, we have access to the throne room of God, through Jesus. So many need to hear this message – who is going to tell them that peace is found in Jesus?

Lord, I ask that you will give me the courage to share this message. Amen

Weddings

We all love a wedding. Friends and family together, good food and drinks, a celebration of love, promises made, the ending of one life and the beginning of a new way of life, as a couple.

Jesus' very first miracle was recorded in John's Gospel. It was at a wedding in Cana. Weddings were a very big event with a huge guest list and lasting for several days. The wine ran out, a nightmare for the event-planner and an embarrassment for the bridegroom! We know that Jesus was a reluctant miracle worker on this particular occasion, he needed some encouragement from his mother. The water of the cleansing jars was changed into the best wine as it was served to the guests. It was a miracle that many shared in, tasting the best of wine and experiencing the lavish supply.

The end of the story of God and his people is also a wedding. 'The Wedding Feast of the Lamb', 'The Great Banquet', 'The Heavenly Banquet', when Jesus comes for his bride. Many of us have missed celebrating Holy Communion, sharing bread and drinking wine together in these days of restrictions, one day, we will celebrate again. Perhaps it will take on greater depth and importance as we journey on? This sharing of bread and wine points us to the new life, the eternal life that God is preparing for us all with the bridegroom, Jesus.

Some words from a liturgy for Holy Communion:

We thank you, Lord, that you have fed us in this sacrament, united us with Christ and given us a foretaste of the heavenly banquet prepared for all people.

Final Flourish

Flourish began in August 2020 – I had asked God if I might ever preach in a church building again, He said I was to "work from home" like others were doing.

God's desire is that we grow and flourish regardless of our circumstances, even a pandemic. I believe many of us have become stronger, kinder and more patient. We have come to realise what is important in life and what is valuable to us, personally. There has been a release of creativity in many areas: art, music, writing, ways of working and ways of reaching out to others. We have been shown the weaknesses in our societies. Situations that are morally and ethically wrong have been revealed. Thousands of lives have been lost and others crippled, physically and mentally. The world's pain is real. The suffering is real. The Christian Church, as well as other faith groups, have provided food for thousands in need. Volunteers have kept our country going, much of it behind the scenes, unknown people of all ages doing what they can. It has been very humbling to see and experience.

A few years ago, I was sorting through some photographs of my parents, our son's nana and granda. I was throwing out pictures that I didn't like. My son then said to me, "Mum, you can't sanitise your past!" as I threw away a seaside picture of his granda in his vest!

The Cross

I wonder if we do that with the crucifixion of Jesus? It is so much easier to ignore the brutality and horror of that event we call Good Friday. The day when Jesus wore a crown of thorns and a cross. Have we sanitised the cross? Jesus is the Lamb of God who takes away the sins of the world, all our sins for all time. Jesus said on the cross, "It is Finished". He completed everything that the Father had told him to do. He fulfilled the job description. He was free to give up his Spirit and return home.

People really do need to hear this story of Jesus, who will tell it?